DEDICATION

To all my grandchildren.
We have shared many happy
moments on the farm.

A Country Christmas
ISBN 1-892728-08-7
Copyright © 1999 by
Georgene Pearson
Route 1, Box 124
Oologah, Oklahoma 74053

Published by
PHOS PUBLISHING, INC.
P. O. Box 690447
Tulsa, Oklahoma 74169-0447

"GRANDMA, how will Santa ever find us this Christmas on the farm?" asked three-year-old Bobbie on a cold winter day as Grandma read her another Christmas story.

"Santa is like LOVE, Darling," said Grandma. "He is everywhere. He'll find us because Santa loves farms too."

She knew Christmas was coming. There were Christmas shows on television and the stores were full of toys. Grandpa had even turned on the lights on the big Christmas tree in the circle drive.

Bobbie's mother, daddy and five-year-old brother, John, had just moved to the dairy farm where Grandpa and Grandma lived. John liked being with Grandpa and was a good little helper. John sometimes thought his sister was such a silly girl.

Bobbie was a very small girl, but she was quick and snappy. Light brown curls framed her face and soft brown eyes twinkled with mischief. She loved all the baby farm animals, especially the baby kittens and the farm dog, Dink.

Later as they walked to the barn, Bobbie exclaimed, "I just looooove this farm."

Grandma smiled as she poured milk into the pan. Bobbie knelt down and watched the kittens little red tongues quickly lap up the milk.

"They are getting milk on their whiskers, Grandma," she snickered.

"That is all right. Their mother will give them a bath when they are finished," assured Grandma as she troked Tuxedo on the head and down her back.

"Does Santa love kittens, too?" Bobbie asked seriously.

"I am sure he does. He loves all the farm animals," answered Grandma.

"Let's go see the other babies, Grandma," she pleaded. "In my storybook there were farm animals in the barn where Jesus was born too."

"We will have to be quiet and not scare them," warned Grandma.

As Sugar Baby, the little pony, looked out from her stall, Bobbie slipped into the pen where Sweet Pea was snuggled in the hay with Dolly and Molly, the twin lambs. They were always ready to play. Bobbie gave Dolly a big hug.

"We know Jesus loves all the baby animals so Santa must love them too," said Grandma smiling. She loved watching Bobbie hug them all.

"That is why you know Santa will come to the farm for Christmas, isn't it?" asked Bobbie shaking her head. Her big eyes twinkled with excitement.

"Will Santa bring presents to the baby calves?" asked Bobbie. Not waiting for an answer, she romped out of the calf barn where Dink, the collie dog, had been waiting.

Grandma was thinking about the question when Bobbie popped her head back inside the barn. "Well, will he, Grandma?" she asked.

"I suppose he will. He will come to see all the animals and you too. Don't you think so?" replied Grandma.

"Sure I do!" Bobbie's shrill voice faded as she bounced back outside to play with Dink who was waiting patiently.

Grandma insisted it was time to go to the dairy barn and get the bottles for the baby calves. So Bobbie dashed down the path, and burst into the milk barn to ask Grandpa a serious question.

"Now what's bothering you, Sugar?" Grandpa asked.

Careful not to get too close to the big milk cows, she asked, "Grandpa, will Santa come to the dairy farm for Christmas?"

"Sure he will, Sugar. He wouldn't miss seeing you for nothin'." Grandpa chuckled as he spoke. "These old cows will be so glad to see Santa, they will probably give eggnog!"

Bobbie doubled up with laughter, "Now Grandpa," she squealed as she reached over and snatched off his old barn cap. "They only give milk, Grandpa!"

John interrupted her laughter with his know-it-all comment. "Everyone knows Santa can find us, wherever we are," he yelled as he was going to get another bucket of feed for the cows. He shook his head thinking about his silly sister.

As Christmas got closer Bobbie told the dog, Dink, that Santa was coming to the farm for Christmas.

She even went to the horse stall to tell Grandpa's horse, Zipper, about Christmas. "Christmas is coming and Santa is coming soon," she whispered in Zipper's ear.

Zipper just nickered as if he wanted some more feed.

Finally Christmas Eve arrived. Bobbie and Grandma went to the calf barn to feed the baby kittens and the small calves. Grandma heard her whispering to all of them. "It is Christmas Eve so Santa's comin' tonight. He will bring you some treats," she promised them.

As Bobbie held the bottle for Sweet Pea she tapped her on her wet nose saying over and over, "Santa is comin' tonight, Santa is comin' tonight."

It was getting much darker now. The evening chores were finished. The big metal Christmas tree that Grandpa had made glistened in the yard with the red, yellow, blue and green lights.

Bobbie and John played tag around the huge Christmas tree in the center of the circle driveway. They were running, laughing and having fun in the new fallen snow until their mother called, "John, Bobbie, it is time to come in for supper."

They went right to the house because Santa would know if they were naughty or nice!

When it was time to go to bed, Bobbie was almost too excited to sleep. She didn't want to miss one single thing tonight. Santa was coming to the farm.

As she said her good night prayer asking Jesus to bless all her family she finished by adding, "And don't forget, Jesus, to tell Santa to come to the farm."

After being tucked into her bed she drifted off to sleep.

It seemed only a minute until she heard noises outside. She jumped out of bed and ran to the window and pulled back the curtains. She could not believe her eyes. Santa and his reindeer had just landed out by the Christmas tree!

Bobbie dashed out the door and ran across the yard. Outside it was as light as if it were day. Santa stepped out of the sleigh. He wasn't surprised to see Bobbie. "I was just hoping to see you. Ho, Ho, Ho," he chuckled and his fat belly jiggled just like the storybook had said. It looked like a bowl full of jelly.

"I was afraid you wouldn't find us at the farm," Bobbie said excitedly, "but I really hoped you would. I have told all the baby animals that you were coming."

"I wouldn't miss coming to the farm at Christmas. Come, let's go to the barn. I have some treats for your little friends," Santa explained.

He had a big brown pack full of toys thrown over his back. White fur trimmed his bright red suit and hat. Black boots came up to his knees. He had a snow-white beard and rosy red cheeks. His eyes twinkled with laughter.

Santa and Bobbie walked toward the big red barn.

"I have a story to tell you when we get there," he said softly after he closed the two steel gates.

"Oh, Santa, I want you to see my baby calves and lambs too," Bobbie said anxiously, "and Snowball, my favorite little kitty."

"That is a cute kitten, Bobbie. Let's go inside and see the other babies."

So they stepped inside the dark barn. Santa pulled the string to turn on the light.

Sugar Baby nickered a welcome as they came into the barn. "You know what, Sugar Baby looks a lot like the little donkey that carried Mary to Bethlehem where Jesus was born," Santa said.

Then he took out some red and white sugar cubes from his pack. One by one he placed them in Bobbie's hand. Sugar Baby whinnied softly as she ate each one.

Bobbie led Santa by the hand to the pens where the baby calves and lambs were sleeping.

The calves were nestled in their beds of hay so Santa tied a silver bell on every pen. He had two red bells, one for Dolly, and one for Molly.

As Bobbie watched she remembered her secret Christmas wish for a necklace with a silver bell.

Bobbie pointed to the next pen and said, "We can sit down here with this baby calf. Her name is Panda Bear and she is very gentle."

"I could use some rest," said Santa as they sat down together on a bale of hay. The baby calf opened her soft black eyes and swished her tail.

As Bobbie snuggled close to Santa, he reached out and patted Panda Bear on the head.

"This reminds me of the first Christmas. There was no room for Mary and Joseph so the innkeeper said they could sleep in the stable barn. That night baby Jesus was born right there with the cows, calves, sheep and donkeys."

"Just like here in our barn?" asked Bobbie not meaning to interrupt.

"Yes, just like it is here. There was no bed for the new baby so Mary, His mother, just wrapped Him in some long strips of cloth and laid Him in a hay manger."

"Our baby calves have a hay manger too," she said pointing to the iron manger in the pen.

His manger bed was made of wood. It wasn't as big and strong as this one," he said.

"I have a picture of Mary and Joseph and baby Jesus in my storybook," Bobbie told Santa.

"I wish the man had let Mary and Joseph sleep in his house," Bobbie said sadly. "So do I," agreed Santa.

"I wouldn't want to sleep in a barn, would you?" Bobbie asked seriously. "No, I wouldn't either," answered Santa. "Now Jesus wants to live in our hearts. We have to make room for him there and not turn Him away like the innkeeper."

"Did you know, Bobbie, that everything we enjoy at Christmas tells us about the Christ child? The evergreen Christmas trees with their lights help to remind us of the life of Jesus, Who is the Light of the world.

"The beautiful angels took the news of the baby to the shepherds while they were out in the fields watching their sheep.

"The bright star led the wise men from the east to the child.

"The round Christmas wreath tells us there is no end to the circle of God's love.

"The ringing of bells makes our Christmas music beautiful.

"The tasty candy cane is shaped like a shepherd's staff and the letter 'J' is to be the secret symbol of Jesus. The red and white stripes remind us of God's Christmas gift to the world.

"That is why we give gifts at Christmas."

"I like your story, Santa, it will always help me to remember the first Christmas story," Bobbie said softly.

"I must be going now," Santa remarked. "Other children are waiting. You know I wouldn't have this good job delivering toys to all the children if Jesus had not been born."

"We have some milk and cookies by the fireplace. I'll be right back," Bobbie said as she jumped up. She dashed down the path past the reindeer and ran toward the house.

Santa latched the gate, turned out the light in the barn and chuckled to himself as he hurried back to his sleigh. He was surprised to find that Grandpa was up early to milk and had given hay to all the reindeer. "I thank you, Sir, and my reindeer thank you too," Santa said as he climbed into his sleigh.

"Santa, Santa," Bobbie shouted almost out of breath, "wait, I have cookies for you."

"Oh, thank you, Bobbie." Reaching into his pack he handed Bobbie a small black box. "And here is a gift for you."

Bobbie opened the box and pulled out the most beautiful gift. In her tiny hand was Rudolph's silver bell tied on a long red and white ribbon. "Oh, thank you, Santa," was all she had time to say.

"Ho, Ho, Ho," Santa chuckled, then he whistled to his team. "On Dasher, on Dancer, on Prancer, on Vixen. On Comet, Cupid, Doner and Blitzen!"

She heard Santa shout as he flew over the farm, "Merry Christmas to all and to all a good night."

"Bye, Santa, I am so glad you came to the farm," she shouted back at him.

"Bobbie, Bobbie. Wake up," cried John. "There are presents under the tree. Come and see."

She bounced out of bed and followed John to the Christmas tree. "Santa did come to the farm. I saw him," she squealed.

"You did?" asked John in surprise. "Where?"

"Out in the yard at the Christmas tree. We went to the barn and he told me the story about the first Christmas too," she insisted.

"Really? Why didn't you wake me up then," John mocked, shaking his head at his silly sister. He thought to himself, *Bobbie must have been dreaming.*

"Let's get Mama and Daddy so we can open our presents."

There was one special present Bobbie kept looking for. It was Rudolph's silver bell. *Surely I didn't lose it,* she thought to herself. *If I found it, then John would have to believe me.*

Every Christmas, Bobbie still hopes to find that necklace with the little silver bell that Santa gave her that Christmas on the farm.

ABOUT THE ILLUSTRATOR

Marjorie Morrow Anderson is a well-known artist in Oklahoma where she has been painting for nearly 40 years. Marjorie has received recognition throughout the United States. One of her paintings was purchased by and promoted through Home Interiors for their catalogue, resulting in over 140,000 prints being sold.

Marjorie is a self-taught artist whose favorite subject matter is children. This love of children has taken her to many countries where she has photographed their universal innocence. The film memories help her to capture them on canvas.

Her travels have also inspired many of the settings of her paintings. Marjorie says her "paintings come from God," since they express the love she feels for the beauty she sees in God's world.

Many of Marjorie's award-winning works are available on Note Cards and Framed Prints and are sold internationally through her Webpage HTTP://hometown.aol.com/marcnart/index.htm Marjorie also authored a book entitled, *You Can Paint Children*.